LITTLE DREAMER

LITTLE DREAMER

NELL JONES

XULON PRESS

Xulon Press
2301 Lucien Way #415
Maitland, FL 32751
407.339.4217
www.xulonpress.com

Printed in the United States of America.

Edited by Xulon Press

ISBN-13: 978-1-54565-818-5

ACKNOWLEDGEMENTS

Coral Foss, affection for your students and the terms of endearment you spoke over them are timeless and precious.

Michelle, this is a book about amazing people just like you. You did not have the opportunity to finish your education and go to college. No one knows just what career you would have chosen if you had. We just know that, at such a young age you taught us so very much and we are grateful.

Mom, you inspired me to write. Dad, you inspired me to study and learn. Bernice, you inspired me to succeed. Thank you!

Lana and Sean. I tried out so many stories on you two. Most of them put you to sleep … but hey, that was ok!

Dayne, I love the way you brought my characters to life.

Sweet, you are my amazing Friend and Mentor.

Xulon, Dixie and Jerolyn: You all taught me not to fear change.

Lynn and Mabel, your listening ears are so appreciated!

Haley, Jake and Bandit: You guys are the best!

I purposely chose to have my characters resemble real people: Terra (Destiny) Keitha (Miss Amelia) Liam (Paxton) and Bob (Ambroise Lefleur). Paxton, thank-you for sharing your name!

TABLE OF CONTENTS

ONE

IMAGINATION FIELD TRIP

One lovely spring day, a bright, imaginative first grader sat quietly at her desk, daydreaming. What will I be when I grow up? she wondered.

Closing her eyes, she saw a huge concert hall full of lights. On stage she saw a shiny grand piano and heard herself playing beautiful, melodious music. The audience below clapped with delight.

All at once, the music stopped. There came a roar so thunderous that it shook the whole stage and made her jump. Cautiously, she peered out from between her fingers. Never had she seen anything like this before.

roarrr!!!

"Yowza!" said the girl in amazement. Through a little round window she saw stars, hundreds of them. A fiery meteor flew by so fast and close, it made her duck.

"Another perfect climb into orbit for Space Shuttle Vision and its six-member crew, on their way to the International Space Station," someone on the radio said.

"I'm an astronaut!" said the girl in amazement. Tightening her seat belt, she looked around. Space was beautiful in a scary sort of way.

A real foot pressed hard up against the back of Little Dreamer's seat. It interrupted her imaginary space flight, bringing her back suddenly.

"Pay attention!" someone whispered. The first grader looked up just in time to see her teacher coming.

"Little D," said Miss Amelia, looking right at her. "What animal is yellow with dark spots and lives in a zoo?"

"A cheetah?" Little D answered, hoping for the best.

"And a giraffe," said Miss Amelia, satisfied. She walked back up front.

"You're welcome," whispered the voice that belonged to the foot.

Little D grinned, but her mind wandered off, once again. And where did she find it next? In the zoo! Beside her stood a little gray hippo. It nudged her with its big wet nose and she just couldn't resist giving it a hug.

"Only your Mom could love you more," she said. Mother hippo was watching, but didn't mind. She trusted Little D with her baby.

TWO

DETERMINATION

Busy sirens screamed past the classroom window. First came a policeman on his way to answer a call. Next came the firetruck with paramedics close behind. Miss Amelia stopped teaching and walked over to the window.

"God, bless the people who need help," she said. After a moment of silence, she continued with her lesson.

Little D looked up at her teacher. What a kind person she is, thought the little girl to herself. Sometimes, sitting still and listening was a hard thing for her to do. But Miss Amelia made it a little easier.

Morning recess came, and everybody put their work away. Outside, Little D sat down on a bench to think. To her surprise, Miss Amelia came and sat beside her.

"You have been taking a lot of imagination field trips lately, haven't you?" her teacher said. Little D was quiet. She didn't know how to answer.

Miss Amelia continued, "Would you like to share what is on your mind?"

"Miss Amelia," answered Little D, "how old were you when you first knew what you wanted to be when you grew up?"

"It took me a while to decide," said the teacher. "First, I wanted to be a nurse and help sick people get well again."

Little D's eyes brightened. "That would be good," she said.

"Then, I decided I wanted to play music and make people happy."

"I thought about that, too," said the little girl. "Did you ever think that you wanted to be an astronaut?"

"Yes, I dreamed of being an astronaut and flying high through space," said Miss Amelia, as she threw her arms up high into the air.

"Why did you change your mind?" asked the little girl.

"I thought I might get homesick," said her teacher sheepishly.

"Or altitude sick," suggested Little D. They both laughed together at that not-so-funny thought!

"I finally decided, though," said Miss Amelia, "teaching was the best job for me." Little D looked into her teacher's eyes.

Miss Amelia continued. "You see, as a teacher I can train little astronauts, computer specialists, nurses, scientists, doctors and..."

"Teachers!" added Little D, excitedly.

"Yes, and even teachers," agreed Miss Amelia. "And, I am glad I made that choice!"

"Me too," said Little D smiling.

"Remember one thing, Little D," said Miss Amelia kindly. "Whatever you choose to do, you will need determination!"

"Determination?" asked Little D.

"Yes, determination. Even when you feel like quitting, don't give up! It takes determination to finish what you start."

"Oh," said Little D. She had never heard that word before, but she liked it! Recess ended, but Little D kept on thinking about what Miss Amelia had said.

THREE

LITTLE CABBAGES

Back in class, Miss Amelia sat down. Across the top of her desk were scattered many pictures, protected and held in place by a smooth, clear glass surface. Little D was curious.

"Miss Amelia," she asked. "Where did all these pictures come from?"

"These are my Little Cabbages," said her teacher proudly. "All grown up."

"Am I your Little Cabbage, too?" asked Little D, hoping.

"Of course, you are," answered Miss Amelia and Little D smiled!

Reaching deep into her pocket, the little girl pulled out a picture. "This is for you to keep," she said shyly.

"Why, thank you!" replied her teacher. "I have just the right place to put this!" Opening her wallet, Miss Amelia turned to the picture section. Little D tried to hide her disappointment. She wanted her picture to join the other little cabbages on top of Miss Amelia's desk!

"I have someone I would like for you to meet." said Miss Amelia. "This is Mr. Ambroise Lafleur, my teacher," she said, smiling. "'Mon Petit Chou,' is what he always said to his own Little Cabbages."

Little D saw a kind looking man with a blue checkered shirt and dark glasses. She did not know what to say. She also did not want to say what she was thinking.

"It's hard for you to imagine your teacher being in first grade, isn't it?" Miss Amelia chuckled. "Now, I have something for you too!" Reaching into her drawer, she pulled out a small picture of herself. Little D couldn't believe her eyes.

"I will cherish this always!" she said, holding it close.

Miss Amelia then pointed to a place on her desk Little D had not noticed before. "Look here," she said. Between her roll book and pencil cup, Little D saw someone very familiar. "Who do you think this is?" the teacher asked with a smile.

"That's me!" replied Little D. "But, how did it get there?"

Miss Amelia pulled a little silver camera out of her bag. "I am a photographer and a teacher," she said smiling. Carefully, she slipped the new picture little D had given her inside her wallet, right next to Mr. Ambroise Lafleur. Little D felt very proud! "Now we have two generations of Cabbages!" said Miss Amelia. "Two, and still counting!" This was the best kind of special Little D had ever felt!

"Maybe I will think about becoming a teacher, too," she said.

Miss Amelia smiled. Then she stood up. In her hand was a silver triangle. She tapped it gently with a small silver wand. "Ting," went the musical triangle and everyone looked up.

"Class, when you hear this sound," said Miss Amelia, "it means, time to listen."

"I like that sound," said Little D. "It makes me want to listen." Everyone agreed. Miss Amelia hung it by a dangly cord, beside the reading center window.

FOUR

POLLYWOGS

"Now," said the teacher. "Please remove your spelling books from your desks and tell me, which one of our new bonus words begins with the letter P?"

"Pollywog!" blurted out Little D. She felt a big foot push up against the back of her seat again. It made her smile. She liked that big foot. She also liked the boy it belonged to!

"Pollywog," Miss Amelia repeated, thoughtfully. "Tell me more!"

"Like a tadpole," said Little D. She was glad that she had caught that one!

"And what is a tadpole?" asked Miss Amelia, doing some fishing herself. "Anyone?"

Paxton Jones bent down to tie his shoe. Nobody else answered, so he said, "A tadpole is a little frog that doesn't have its arms and legs yet." Little D smiled at his explanation. Paxton smiled too! There was that foot again. Miss Amelia noticed but pretended not to see!

"Right you both are," said their teacher. All eyes and ears were on Miss Amelia now, waiting to hear what she would say next.

"A pollywog is a baby frog or tadpole," she said. "Most baby frogs begin their lives in the water and must breathe out of gills, just like fish. Then, something really wonderful happens." said their teacher. "Lungs begin to develop, little arms and legs start to grow, it crawls out of the water and...

"jumps onto a rock!" said Miss Amelia, laughing. Everybody else jumped too! "Caught you listening," said their teacher smiling! "Good job. Now, who wants to have recess?"

Little D liked her teacher's stories. Sometimes she liked them too much and didn't want to move on! Whenever her mind began to wander like that, which was quite often, Miss Amelia would simply remind her:

"Imagination field trip is over now; please join us," and that was that!

FIVE

HERE WE GO

Time passed, but Little D didn't notice much. First grade tumbled into second, second slid into third and before she knew it, Little D was feeling right at home in Middle School. Like a butterfly coming out of its cocoon, she just kept on growing and changing. In High School, a pretty, young lady emerged!

"Just call me D," the pretty young lady said with a smile; and that's exactly what everyone did!

In high school, Miss Amelia's picture moved into a new red wallet. It sat in her purse beside a little silver camera just like the one belonging to, well, you know who!

Four years passed, way too fast. "Determined D," as her teachers liked to call her, worked hard but always found time to play a little and to do a good deed.

One spring day, D sat in her high school auditorium surrounded by classmates, friends and family. On her head was a graduation cap. A little tassel dangled just above her right eyebrow. She smoothed her silky blue gown and looked around. On stage a teacher began talking.

"Welcome Graduates," he said. "We are here today to help you celebrate. What you started in first grade, you will now bring to completion, twelve years later." Everybody clapped.

"We call this ceremony Commencement, because you are commencing upon a new and different path. In this audience we could soon have doctors, scientists, musicians, astronauts..."

"And teachers," thought D, smiling at the memory.

"In just a minute," he continued, "your name will be called, and you will walk up on stage to receive your diploma. At that time, you may move the tassel on your cap over to the other side recognizing this great achievement."

One by one the graduates received their diplomas. One by one they moved their tassels to the other side. D waited, then she heard her name. It was her turn.

"Destiny Wren." She felt a push from behind!

"Go!" said a familiar voice and the excited graduate stood up! Across the stage she went to receive her High School Diploma.

"Another Cabbage leaves the patch!" said Miss Amelia who was sitting in the front row cheering. SNAP, went a familiar little camera. D blinked and waved.

"Thank you for believing in me!" she said.

"Always," replied her first-grade teacher.

SIX

NOW WHAT?

"**N**ow what?" asked the eager young lady, but of course she already knew! "Four more years of studies for me," she said.

Off to college she went! D's professors were very kind and willing to help.

"So, you want to be a teacher," they said. "Our question is then, what would you like to teach?" The new college student thought for a minute.

"I could teach P.E.," she said. "Exercise is a good thing." Everyone agreed.

"Music, maybe," came a friendly suggestion.

"I thought about that too," said D, smiling.

"You will learn many things while you are here," they all said. "Listen, study and do your homework. Then you can decide."

Not-So-Little-Now D took their advice. She studied hard, but still found time for fun. Two days a week she helped at the community animal shelter. Three times a week she exercised with her friends in the gym.

She even wrote stories for the campus newspaper. Everyday D went to class expecting to learn something new and she was never disappointed. One spring day a big box arrived. It said,

"Special Delivery for Destiny Wren."

D lifted the lid. Inside, she saw a purple cap and gown. Graduation Day was here. Destiny Wren sighed. She was both happy and sad. The years had gone by so fast. Little thoughts and dreams had turned into one great big plan with lots of expectations. Was she really ready to move on? What did moving on even mean?

Then she remembered her first-grade teacher, Miss Amelia's advice. "Determination, Little D," she had once said. "Even when it gets hard, you don't give up! Finish what you start."

"This is it," she thought. Taking her new cap and gown out of the box, she hung them on her door. "I am really going to be a teacher now," she said.

SEVEN

LOOK HOW FAR WE'VE COME

One more time, graduation day came. One more time, D put on her cap and gown. The little tassel seemed to know its place. Sitting with her classmates, she looked around. There was her family, friends and even – you know who!

"Fellow graduates, four years ago…" said a speaker. Destiny looked up to see her friend from the library. "We came to this place," he continued. "We were excited, but a little scared, remember?" He asked. Everyone nodded. They knew it was true.

"Every day we came to class. Every day, we listened to our professors and did the work they assigned. In fact, we wouldn't be where we are at right now if it wasn't for them." Everybody clapped. The professors clapped too. They looked very distinguished in their caps and gowns.

"We are still excited," said the speaker, "and we are still a little scared, but not as much as before. It is our time now to take what we have been taught and share it. Someone else out there is waiting to hear your story!"

One by one and once again, the students received their diplomas. Then it was D's turn.

"Miss Destiny Joy Wren." said the speaker. Again, this amazing young woman walked across the stage, this time to receive her College Diploma and Teaching Certificate. My, how everyone cheered!

In the audience below, as you know, sat a proud first grade teacher wiping her eyes. Then, pulling a shiny silver camera out of her purse, she snapped a picture, to go under the glass on top of her desk.

"Mon petit chou," she said. "You have done exceedingly well, My Little Cabbage." D smiled and waved.

"I will have little cabbages too!" she said!

"Indeed, you will," said Miss Amelia, smiling.

CPSIA information can be obtained
at www.ICGtesting.com
Printed in the USA
JSHW040702200221
11840JS00008B/117